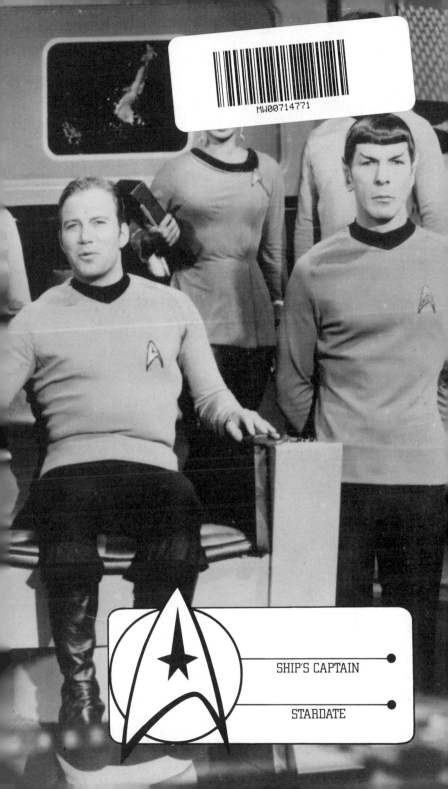

SHIP'S CAPTAIN

STARDATE

"This is all some sort of trap." (Spock — THE CAGE)

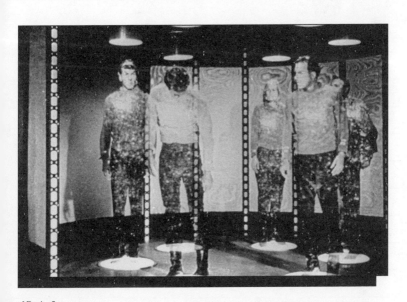

"We'll never reach an Earth base with him [Mitchell] aboard." (Spock – WHERE NO MAN HAS GONE BEFORE)

In MUDD'S WOMEN, Kirk and Spock must replenish the Enterprise's dilithium crystals.　(Trivia)

"Yes, we are very much alike, Captain—both proud of our ships." (Balok—THE CORBOMITE MANEUVER)

"But it's not a duplicate, it's an opposite."

(Scott—THE ENEMY WITHIN)

In THE NAKED TIME, a strange disease infects the crew of the Enterprise. Under its effects, Mr. Sulu threatens the crew.

(Trivia)

"Janice — They can't feel...Not like you...They don't love...Please...I want to stay." (CHARLIE X)

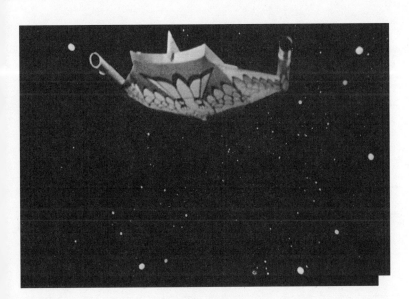

"Open channels, warn that ship off!" (Kirk – BALANCE OF TERROR)

"The android will be so perfect it could even replace the Captain?" (Roger Korby—WHAT ARE LITTLE GIRLS MADE OF?)

"Can you imagine a mind emptied by that thing, without even a tormentor for company." (Kirk — DAGGER OF THE MIND)

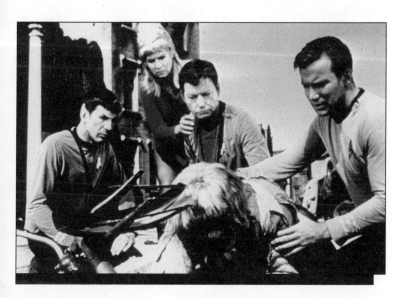

"It's incredible . . . almost as if it aged a century in just the past few minutes." (McCoy-MIRI)

"I have to get back to my ship and figure out how I'm going to enter this into my log." (Kirk — THE CONSCIENCE OF A KING)

"A little less analysis and more action, that's what we need Mr. Spock." (McCoy – THE GALILEO SEVEN)

Captain Kirk's COURT MARTIAL ends when Ben
Finney is found alive aboard the Starship Enterprise.

(Trivia)

"They've reached into my mind and taken the memory of somewhere I've been." (Captain Pike — THE MENAGERIE)

_____

_____

_____

_____

_____

_____

_____

In the ARENA, Kirk had to fight the Gorn in hand-to-hand combat when Metrons transported both to the planet surface. (Trivia)

_____

_____

_____

_____

_____

In THE ALTERNATIVE FACTOR, the "nonexistence effect" was experienced throughout the universe when Lazarus caused a dimensional corridor to open in time.

(Trivia)

In THE RETURN OF THE ARCHONS, Spock
encounters the image of Landru.

(Trivia)

In A TASTE OF ARMAGEDDON, the planet Eminiar VII has been at war with its neighbor Vendikar for centuries. The "war" is fought by computers that estimate the number of casualties anticipated and then that number of people is executed. (Trivia)

"The trip is over, the battle begins again, only this time it's not a world to win, it's a universe."   (Kahn—SPACE SEED)

In THIS SIDE OF PARADISE, Spock is affected by an alien plant's spores and for the first time is able to experience happiness and human emotions. (Trivia)

"Go out into the tunnel to The Chamber of The Ages. Cry for the children, walk carefully in the vault of tomorrow."

(Spock — DEVIL IN THE DARK)

"I am the Guardian of Forever . . . I am my own beginning, and my own ending." (Guardian of Forever-City on THE EDGE OF FOREVER)

"Set your phasers on force 3, to kill."

(Kirk — OPERATION: ANNIHILATE!)

Although it appears to be outdoors, Apollo's temple in WHO MOURNS FOR ADONAIS, was built on an indoor set. (Trivia)

In AMOK TIME, Spock experiences "pon farr," the Vulcan mating cycle, and has to return to his planet to take a wife. Spock must fight Kirk for the woman he is to marry.

(Trivia)

"Cold (the creature) was, like a stinking draft out of a slaughter house." (Mr. Scott – WOLF IN THE FOLD)

_____

_____

_____

_____

_____

_____

_____

In THE CHANGELING, Nomad, an old Earth space probe, confused James T. Kirk with its creator Jackson Roykirk.

(Trivia)

_____

_____

_____

_____

_____

In THE DEADLY YEARS the crew is exposed to a strange
disease which causes rapid aging.   (Trivia)

Ensign Pavel Chekov, seen here in I, MUDD, did not join the Enterprise crew until the second season of Star Trek.

(Trivia)

_____

_____

_____

_____

_____

_____

THE TROUBLE WITH TRIBBLES episode made the
furry Tribbles — "the only love money can buy" — very
popular.   (Trivia)

_____

_____

_____

_____

_____

"Those who could adapt lived; those who couldn't died in the arena."

(Captain Merik—BREAD AND CIRCUSES)

Because it introduced Mr. Spock's parents, Sarek and Amanda, JOURNEY TO BABEL is one of Star Trek's most popular episodes. EL)

(Trivia)

"Jim's been poisoned by a [deadly] Mugatu."

(McCoy—A PRIVATE LITTLE WAR)

"I am Galt, the master thrall . . . You are to be trained and spend the rest of your lives here." (Galt—THE GAMESTERS OF TRISKELION)

"Do you think you know what it was Captain?" (Spock)
"Something that couldn't possibly exist, but it does."(Kirk—OBSESSION)

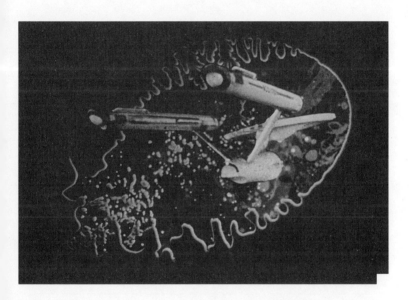

"It's a disease, like a virus invading the body of our galaxy." (McCoy—THE IMMUNITY SYNDROME)

In A PIECE OF THE ACTION, Spock and Dr. McCoy
hold the crime bosses of the planet Iotia captive while
Kirk takes over.   (Trivia)

In BY ANY OTHER NAME Spock uses the Vulcan mind meld to plant a suggestion in the mind of a Kelvan.

(Trivia)

In RETURN TO TOMORROW, Sargon, one of three survivors from Arret, is allowed to invade Kirk's body in order to construct permanent android bodies. (Trivia)

"Your uniform, Captain. You should make a very convincing Nazi." (Spock—PATTERNS OF FORCE)

"Scotty, lock in on our position."

(Kirk—ASSIGNMENT: EARTH)

"In THE OMEGA GLORY, Kirk, Spock, and McCoy are exposed to a deadly virus and need to find a cure before they return to the Enterprise.

(Trivia)

Kirk finds that THE ULTIMATE COMPUTER has taken control of the Enterprise. (Trivia)

The Troyian Ambassador has little success in teaching social graces to the Dohlman of Elas in ELAAN OF TROYIUS. (Trivia)

In THE PARADISE SYNDROME, Kirk loses his memory and becomes Kirok, the leader of an Indian Tribe. (Trivia)

"The readings do not correlate with any known information."

(Spock—AND THE CHILDREN WILL LEAD)

McCoy uses "the Teacher" to gain the knowledge to replace Spock's brain, in SPOCK'S BRAIN. (Trivia)

"I would appreciate an opportunity to exchange greetings with the ambassador." (Spock — IS THERE IN TRUTH NO BEAUTY?)

"She is saving herself. She does not yet have the instinct to save her people." (Vian — THE EMPATH)

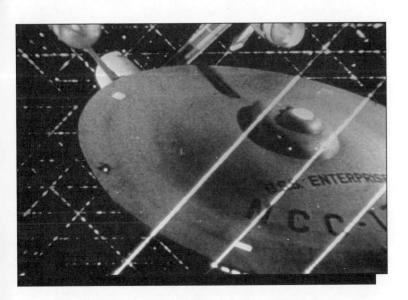

" . . . and if the Tholians are successful in completing this structure before we have completed our repairs, we shall not see home again.

(Spock—THE THOLIAN WEB)

"Kirk and Spock have committed sacrilege. You know what must be done."

(Oracle—FOR THE WORLD IS HOLLOW AND I HAVE TOUCHED THE SKY)

PLATO'S STEPCHILDREN featured the first interracial
kiss on Network Television.

(Trivia)

"There was no force field. Something shoved me back."

(Kirk — WINK OF AN EYE)

"Energize."

(Kirk — THAT WHICH SURVIVES)

"I am black on the right side."

(Bele—LET THAT BE YOUR LAST BATTLEFIELD)

In WHOM GODS DESTROY, Kirk and Spock bring a new drug to an asylum that has been taken over by its inmates.

(Trivia)

"We must acknowledge once and for all that the purpose of diplomacy is to prolong crisis. (Spock—THE MARK OF GIDEON)

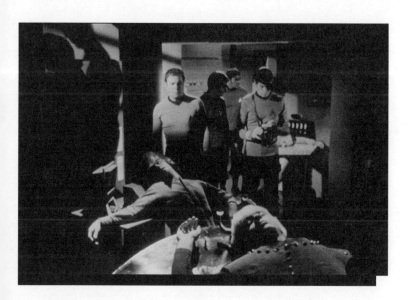

In THE LIGHTS OF ZETAR, an energy storm destroys all the inhabitants of Memory Alpha, the central library facility of the United Federation of Planets.

(Trivia)

In THE CLOUDMINDERS, the miners live on the planet's harsh surface while the ruling class — Stratos-dwellers — inhabit the luxurious city above the planet.

(Trivia)

In THE WAY TO EDEN, The Enterprise beams aboard the crew of the Aurora right before the ship explodes, and encounters their brilliant but insane leader Dr. Sevrin.

(Trivia)

_____

_____

_____

_____

_____

_____

_____

In REQUIEM FOR METHUSELAH, Kirk, Spock, and McCoy meet Flint, a man who has lived for thousands of years and has collected many of Earth's treasures to fill his loneliness. (Trivia)

_____

_____

_____

_____

_____

In THE SAVAGE CURTAIN, a rock creature named Yarnek threatens to destroy the Enterprise. (Trivia)

TURNABOUT INTRUDER, the last original Star Trek episode, aired June 3, 1969. (Trivia)

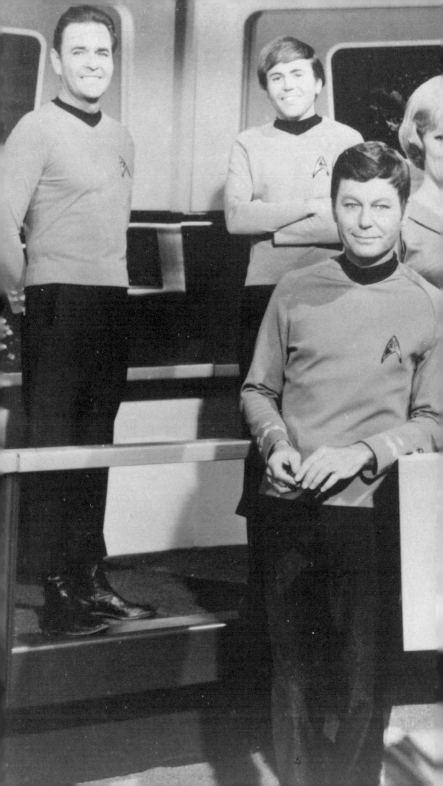